Also by Jo Simmons

Super Loud Sam

Pip Street: The Great Kitty Kidnap

Pip Street: The Crazy Crumpet Kerfuffle

Pip Street: The Pesky Pig Panic

Pip Street: The Big Brother Bother

SUPER LOUD SAM vs BIRDMAN

Jo Simmons

SCHOLASTIC

Scholastic Children's Books
An imprint of Scholastic Ltd
Euston House, 24 Eversholt Street, London, NW1 1DB, UK
Registered office: Westfield Road, Southam, Warwickshire, CV47 0RA
SCHOLASTIC and associated logos are trademarks and/
or registered trademarks of Scholastic Inc.
First published in the UK by Scholastic Ltd, 2016

Text copyright © Jo Simmons, 2016
Illustration copyright © Tom Knight, 2016

The right of Jo Simmons and Tom Knight to be identified as the author
and illustrator of this work has been asserted by them.

ISBN 978 1407 15231 8

A CIP catalogue record for this book
is available from the British Library.

Printed by CPI Group (UK) Ltd, Croydon, CR0 4YY
Papers used by Scholastic Children's Books are made
from wood grown in sustainable forests.

1 3 5 7 9 10 8 6 4 2

www.scholastic.co.uk

TO MY BOYS.
YES, GEORGE, YOU CAN HAVE SOME CEREAL.
NO, DYLAN, YOU CAN'T HAVE A PUG.

Chapter 1
PECK UP A PICNIC

"YUCK!" yelled Sam.

Sam's friend Nina flinched at the noise. She couldn't help it. Sam Lowe was just so loud: a dinky little dude with a massive voice. People used to find Sam's voice annoying, until he showed them how awesome it was. It could be heard ten streets away (who needs a mobile?). It could form a sonic shock wave and blast objects out of the way. It could make grown men spill tea down their fronts in surprise. See? Awesome.

It was more than a voice, it was a power: a superpower! Because Sam Lowe was also Super Loud (with capital letters, thank you very much), the hero who just a few weeks ago had defeated his dangerous, noise-hating teacher Mrs Sandy Mann, and saved the children of Topside from a life filled with no fun.

For the moment, though, Sam was just being Sam, enjoying the summer holidays with his best friend Nina. Right now they were having a picnic in Topside Park.

"BLUURRGGHH! I HATE

WOOLLY PEARS!" Sam blasted. He

spat out a mouthful of fluffy fruit.

"Woolly pears, nature's cares," said Nina.
Nina had a habit of speaking in weird Zen-
master riddles. Sam mostly ignored it. "What
else don't you like?" Nina asked.

"Woolly pants," said Sam. "Too itchy!"

Nina giggled quietly. "I *really* love knitting," she said, "but even I would never knit a pair of woolly pants." In fact, as Nina spoke, she was knitting an extension to the woolly rug the children were sitting on. Somehow she was nibbling a cheese sandwich at the same time.

"Too-tight pants," said Sam. "Broccoli, obviously. And I don't like brushing my teeth if I have my coat on, either. It feels really..." He trailed off as something had caught his eye.

"Weird," he said, pointing over Nina's shoulder.

There were some pigeons on the grass. Nothing odd about that, you might think.

Parks are full of pigeons. Towns are full of pigeons. The whole country is full of pigeons.

Only, these particular pigeons were standing in a neat row, staring sternly at Sam and Nina. They didn't move. They just stared. When did you ever see pigeons do that?

Then, suddenly, they took off, flew high in the air, gathered speed and height, turned and...

"FLIPPING FLIP HECK!" roared Sam. **"THEY'RE COMING STRAIGHT FOR US! RUN!"**

Sam and Nina scrambled to their feet and scattered as the line of birds dived, like a squadron of fighter planes, at their picnic.

They swooped over the cheese sandwiches and crisps and chocolate fingers and pears, scooped them up in their claws – and then dropped them like bombs.

Again and again, the pigeons dived, swooped, grabbed and dropped. Sam and Nina watched, wide-eyed, from behind a tree.

"HEY!" bawled Sam in his massive voice.

"LEAVE OFF OUR SARNIES!"

Lummy! That shout was loud, but the picnic-pilfering pigeons ignored Sam's exceptional outburst. Were they deaf? Or just really tough? Impossible to say.

Finally, the bad-news birds flew off and the children returned to their picnic. What a mess! It was destroyed: food scattered everywhere, Nina's knitted rug ripped and shredded.

"I thought pigeons were meant to be thick, but these guys seemed to know exactly what they were doing," said Sam, surveying the scene.

"Actually," said Nina, "pigeons are quite bright. They can recognize their reflection in a mirror, and even learn to play ping-pong."

"This wasn't exactly ping-pong, though, was it?" said Sam. "They deliberately wrecked our picnic."

The children gathered up the remains of their meal and blanket and dumped it all in the bin.

"OoOF!" exploded Sam as they were walking away.

Something had hit him on the head. Something soft and damp. He looked up to see one of the pigeons that had demolished the picnic flying off. Then Sam looked down to see what had struck him. There, lying on the grass a little way off, were the remains of the woolly pear!

"YUCK AGAIN!" shouted Sam.

Nina looked serious. "When fruit is falling," she said, "dark days are calling."

"If you say so," Sam shrugged. "Let's go home before I get hit by something nastier than fruit."

Chapter 2
BIRDS BEHAVING BADLY

Over the next few days, Sam and Nina noticed

several other peculiar pigeon events. They

saw three pigeons stealing sun hats from

a group of old folks who were snoozing in

deckchairs in Topside Park. That's no way to

treat senior citizens, is it? Another time, Sam

and Nina spotted pigeons picking up bits of

litter – mushy chips, banana skins, empty

drinks cartons – and dropping them on people

walking along the street below. Sam yelled in

his toppest of topmost voices, but that only scared the people half out of their skins, while the pigeons just looked at Sam as if to say, "Really?"

On top of these mean misdeeds, pigeons were up to all kinds of clever stuff, too. One afternoon Sam and Nina were walking to meet Sam's mum, Jen, where she worked at a local hairdressers, Prime Cuts. Suddenly, Sam let out a huge shout.

"A PIGEON JUGGLING!" he boomed. **"OVER THERE!"**

"What with?" asked Nina.

"I dunno, peas or something," said Sam.

"Peas?" said Nina. "Where's he going to find peas? Peas don't grow on trees, you know."

"What do they grow on?" asked Sam.

"They grow underground, I think," said Nina.

"No, you're thinking of pea*nuts*," said Sam. "Anyway, I know what I saw. A pigeon juggling! What is it with pigeons at the moment?"

Sam told his mum what he had seen as they all walked home.

"What's a pigeon going to juggle with?" she also asked.

"I don't know!" exploded Sam. "But I know what I saw."

"He said it was peas," whispered Nina.

"A pigeon juggling peas?" Sam's mum laughed. "Garden peas or petits pois?"

Nina giggled, but Sam had the last laugh when the three of them sat down after dinner to watch *Talking Topside*, the local news programme. . .

Chapter 3

TUNING IN TO TALKING TOPSIDE

It was six-thirty p.m., and *Talking Topside* had just begun. There was a picture of a pigeon behind the newsreader, Martin Streaky.

"Topside's pigeons are behaving out of character," he said. "Town residents have sighted them performing a flock of naughty acts, causing widespread distress. Here's Tess Trotter with the birdie briefing. . ."

"IT'S TOPSIDE PARK!" shouted Sam, pointing at the TV. The camera panned around the park, then went up close on a group of pigeons pecking the ground.

"It's a familiar scene," said the reporter. "Pigeons enjoying a snack of cake crumbs at the local park café. In fact, it's so familiar that most of us hardly notice pigeons from one day to the next. But all that looks set to change. Pigeons, it seems, are getting smarter! A number of eyewitness accounts report pigeons boxing, doing somersaults and even juggling!"

"TOLD YOU!" exploded Sam, rattling the windows with his mighty shout.

"Sshhh," said Nina, "there's more."

"Unfortunately, the birds are not content to

stop there. They are also causing havoc across the town with their anti-social behaviour," Tess Trotter went on. She turned to a group of young mothers, each holding a squirming toddler.

"We were sitting on rugs, with lots of bricks and toys laid out," said one of the mothers, "when about twenty pigeons flew down and chased us away. Then they kicked over the bricks, which really upset all the children."

"Can you describe the pigeons to me?" asked Tess Trotter.

"Grey feathers, two wings, small eyes, a beak," said the mother. "Actually, they looked bigger than ordinary pigeons. They were definitely scarier."

"How did you feel when the pigeons attacked?" asked the reporter.

"The children were crying and screaming," said the mother. "We were very frightened."

Right on cue, one toddler started wailing, then another and another, as if reliving the scary event.

Tess Trotter turned to face the camera, the mums and crying tots behind her. Sam spotted a man carrying a big backpack at the edge of the group. He paused to watch the filming, cocking his head slightly to one side as he did so.

"Keep your eyes peeled for more pigeon peculiarities," said Tess Trotter, having to shout over the noise of wailing infants. "You can email the show or tweet us using the hashtag #pigeonfancythat. We will be running a regular Pigeon Post feature in the news every night and reporting your stories of pigeon activity. This is Tess Trotter, at the park, with some noisy babies, for *Talking Topside*. Back to you in the studio, Martin."

Chapter 4
EXPERT ALERT!

"I can't believe it!" said Sam's mum once the news report from the park had finished.

"I know, pigeons hassling innocent little kids," said Sam.

"No!" said Sam's mum. "I can't believe I cut that woman's hair just the other day. Didn't realize she worked on the local news."

On the TV, Martin Streaky was now talking to bird expert Phil Noddy. "Phil, you are a bird expert and know about birds. Can you explain this strange, aggressive pigeon behaviour?" he asked.

"To be honest, Martin, it's all very odd," said Phil Noddy, frowning. "I have never come across this kind of behaviour before, certainly not in pigeons."

"The mother in the park there said the birds seemed bigger than normal pigeons," said Martin Streaky.

"That's right," said Phil Noddy. "I have studied a photo that one of the mums took of these pigeons and they look at least a third bigger, with really quite powerful wings, tough beaks and strong feet."

"Should we be worried?" asked Martin Streaky.

"Possibly," said Phil Noddy. "Topside alone has a huge pigeon population. If every pigeon in the town grew this big and began to act aggressively, we could have a major problem.

If this bird behaviour spread beyond Topside, I'm not sure how we could cope. Think about the massive number of pigeons currently living throughout the UK! If they all started attacking, they could turn our towns and cities into no-go zones."

"That's a worrying thought," said Martin Streaky.

"Yes it is," said Phil Noddy.

Sam frowned. The worrying thought was indeed worrying, and Sam felt worried. And full of questions, too. Why would pigeons suddenly be bigger? And what was prompting them to act smarter but also meaner?

Nina obviously felt the same. She had that

Zen-master faraway look in her eye. "When cats bark at dogs, the moon shall jump over the sun," she muttered.

Sam frowned but, for once, he kind of knew what she meant.

Chapter 5

SAM AND NiNA TRY SOME SPYING

Tales of pigeon weirdness spread through Topside like marge on hot toast. Everyone was talking about pigeons and swapping stories about their behaviour. Pigeons had been spotted lifting weights in the park (the weights were AA batteries, but anyway). One pigeon had taken to hiding behind trees and jumping out on sniffing dogs – a pug had needed treatment at the vet's for shock. Another pigeon had flown into someone's kitchen, popped open the fridge and helped itself to a yoghurt.

"Have you noticed something?" Sam said as they watched the Pigeon Post reports on *Talking Topside* one evening. "Him!" Sam pointed to the screen as a man with a large backpack appeared in the background, just briefly. He glanced at the camera, cocked his head, and then walked off with strange, strutting steps. "He is always there when they are filming the pigeons or talking to people about them," said Sam.

Nina broke off from knitting her latest project – a set of soup bowls. "Perhaps he just wants to be famous?" she said.

Sam had been famous after he had defeated

his evil teacher, Mrs Mann, and it had been nice to have the attention. For a while, at least. But then hc was happy for things to go back to normal. In fact, Sam had no idea when he might use his powers again, or whether he even should. His mentor, Bryce Canyon, the coolest speech therapist ever, had disappeared. Without Bryce to check in with, Sam wasn't sure how super he should be.

Sam flicked off the TV and offered to walk Nina home. It was a lovely summer evening, and as the pair started out for Nina's house in the next street, they spotted a *Talking Topside* TV van and rushed after it, eager to find out what pigeon shenanigans it was off to film now.

By the time the children caught up with the van near the train station, Tess Trotter the reporter had finished presenting and was climbing back inside.

"HEY, MY MUM CUT YOUR HAIR!" shouted Sam, extremely loudly. Tess Trotter smiled tightly at him and the van drove off.

"That's gratitude for you," grumbled Nina, but Sam was staring into the distance. He had spotted him again: the backpack man, strutting off after watching the filming, his head bobbing back and forth with each step.

"Come on," said Sam, as quietly as he could manage. "Let's follow him."

So a cat-and-mouse following situation began, with Sam and Nina pursuing the man, crouching behind cars and ducking behind walls whenever he turned round. After a few minutes, they arrived at wasteland near the railway lines and saw the man disappear into an old warehouse.

"Should we go in?" whispered Nina after they had watched for a bit.

"No, look," said Sam. "He's coming out." The man strutted off in the opposite direction. Once they were sure he had gone, the children crept up to the warehouse. The doors were padlocked but Sam found a small window on one side. He opened his mouth and sent out a shock wave of sound: a big rippling tidal wave of noise created deep in his chest. **BOOM!** It easily popped the window out of its frame. Nina then quickly knitted a rope that she threw into the window, and the children climbed through.

Once inside, it took the children a few

moments to adjust to the dim light, but they could hear movement all around. Cooing. Wings flapping. The *trip-trap* of little pink feet. Sam shuddered as he sensed hundreds of tiny eyes peering down at him. It could only mean one thing. . .

Chapter 6
BIRD WORLD

"PIGEONS!" Sam roared. "This place is full of pigeons!"

Correct. There were pigeons everywhere. Imagine a warehouse full of pigeons, then double the number of pigeons and get them to invite their friends over. *That's* how many. They were sitting on the rafters, on the floor and on rows and rows of stands, like fences or barriers, which looked specially designed for perching on. And they were big, too: bigger and tougher than your typical pigeon.

Suddenly, amid all the cooing and feathery fidgeting, the children heard a laugh. From above! They looked up. The man! Still wearing his backpack! He was above them, perched on one of the roof beams. How the heck did he get up there?

"Coo-coo-coo-*cool* to see you, children," he said, before dropping down in front of them. "I was wondering when you would show up, Sam."

"You know my name!" Sam spluttered.

"Of coo-coo-course. I read in the local paper how you defeated your noise-hating teacher with your voice," said the man, cocking his head and blinking at Sam. "Exceptional humans and animals fascinate me."

The man strutted off slowly through the warehouse. Thousands of beady pigeon eyes watched him.

"Coo-coo-coo-could you come over here, children?" he said. "I will open your minds to the truth about pigeons!"

The man pushed open a door and revealed a brightly lit room divided into different areas. The pigeons seemed to get excited and began circling above.

"This is a pigeon playground!" said the

man. "Come my friends, fly down and p-p-p-peck, party and play!"

The birds swooped down and flew inside, the wind from their wingbeats making Sam's floppy blond hair blow about. They landed and began all sorts of activities. There was a games area, where some played ping-pong while others kicked a football the size of a walnut around. Over in the art gallery, pigeons strolled quietly between the paintings, cocking their heads to squint at the pictures of trees and meadows.

"They love landscapes," said the man. "But modern art – not so much."

In the restaurant zone, pigeons could choose treats to eat. Big tanks held cornflakes, raisins, Bombay mix and cherries. The pigeons' favourite was the chocolate chips. A queue had formed, with pigeons lining up to peck the button and receive a choccy cupful.

"Is this how they get to be so big?" Sam asked. "Eating all this food?"

The man did not reply. Instead, he reached over the birds' heads, hit the button and let some chocolate chips tumble into his palm. But instead of raising his hand to his mouth and popping them in, he lowered his head, jabbing at the chips with his mouth, pecking them up and scattering some to the floor.

Sam and Nina gawped, speechless.

"I thought you'd say that!" said the man.

"We haven't said anything," Sam managed to reply.

"Precisely!" said the man. "The truth about how intelligent pigeons are can peck the words right out of your mouth! You thought they were thick, Sam, didn't you? I heard you say that in the park a few days ago."

"When they attacked our picnic? You were there?" spluttered Sam, a shiver running down his spine.

"I like to keep an eye on my birds while they are out and about," said the man. "You coo-coo-coo-can't be sure what kind of people they may come across!"

"So pigeons are actually clever?" asked Sam.

"Oh, yes," said the man, admiring the birds. "Eager to learn, too. That's what this place is all about. It's a school: a training academy for exploring and enhancing the pigeons' natural abilities. People don't appreciate pigeons, but they should."

"The way they have been upsetting people, stealing food and scaring old folks isn't exactly helping everyone to like them," said Sam.

"Oh, people don't need to *like* them, exactly," said the backpack man, "but they should respect them."

He broke off as a large pigeon landed on his

shoulder and did a big white poo on it.

"Err, I think you've been dolloped on," said Sam, pointing at the splat, but the man just raised a hand to silence him.

Seconds later, a group of pigeons carrying a cloth flew down and began wiping up the mess. Then they sponged the area clean and finished by spraying scent on it, before flying off silently.

"You see?" said the man. "Coo-coo-coo-couldn't get a dog to do that!"

"Yeah, but a dog wouldn't climb on to your shoulder and poo on it," said Sam, and then wished he hadn't. The man cocked his head and stared at him with his beady eyes.

"What happens in there?" asked Nina, to distract him. She pointed to a locked door at the end of the room.

The man frowned. "It's private," he said sharply. "Strictly no admittance. You have seen enough now. Off you go. Run along and tell your friends to admire and respect pigeons. The days of these birds being ignored and badly treated are almost over. Remember, someone very clever once said, 'the pigeon is mightier than the sword!'"

"Pen," said Nina. "The pen is mightier than the sword."

"Whatever!" said the man. "Get out!"

Chapter 7
THE PURPOSE OF PIGEONS

The sun was still shining when Sam and Nina left the warehouse, but the shadows had grown long.

"That was ... er ... interesting," said Nina.

"Don't you mean that was totally whizz-bang, off-the-scale, 'like, hello?' weird?" replied Sam.

Nina looked serious. "I suppose there's nothing wrong with being friends with pigeons and helping them to fulfil their potential," she said. She had, after all, always known that these birds were intelligent.

"Yes, but it goes further than that," said Sam. "It's this guy's birds that are hitting the headlines every night on *Talking Topside*, and getting up to all kinds of naughty stuff. He's always there in the background. Seems like he's doing more than just teaching them about art. He said that place is a training academy, but the only thing the pigeons seem to be learning is how to be a nuisance."

"And how to clean poo off people's shoulders," Nina added. "So it's not all bad!"

As Sam and Nina remembered the birds carefully wiping up poop from the man's shoulder, they burst out laughing.

"Maybe they will stop causing trouble in the town and start tidying it up instead," said Nina.

Sam frowned. "It's a nice idea," he said, "but I've got a feeling that this man and his pigeons have plans that go beyond simply spring-cleaning Topside."

Chapter 8
THROUGH THE
BEDROoM WiNDOW

THUD!

Sam wokc with a start. Early morning.
Something had hit his bedroom window. With
his heart pounding, he pulled back the curtain
to look. A pigeon sat on the sill outside, staring
boldly at him. Had it just flown into the glass?
It didn't look stunned. It looked fine. At
close range, Sam could really appreciate how
big it was: much bigger and more dramatic
than a typical pigeon. It had wider wings,

longer toes and a thicker beak.

"Did you hit my window?" Sam asked.

After yesterday's visit to the backpack
man's warehouse academy, where pigeons
were acting in extra-intelligent ways, Sam
half expected the pigeon to reply. But no.
Instead, it gave Sam a look of milk-curdling
indifference, ruffled its feathers and flew off.

What an odd way to start the day, thought Sam,
curling up under his duvet again. His dozy
slumbers were interrupted soon again, though.
A cat was yowling in the garden below. It
sounded like Pig, the cat belonging to his
neighbour, Mrs Frazzle. Sam had no idea why
she'd called her cat "Pig" when he was a cat,

not a pig. He didn't even look like a pig. He looked like a cat.

In fact, right now he looked like a frightened cat. He was being attacked by a band of tough-nut pigeons. The enormous birds swooped down on Pig, trying to peck his tail or wing-bash him, one after another after another. Poor Pig looked utterly outnumbered, crouching on the lawn, hissing and trying to swipe the birds with his paw.

Sam was shocked. He opened the window and shouted at the birds. His shouts were loud and mighty, unlike anything normal humans could produce, but these birds didn't care. They carried on hassling poor Pig. *Right,* thought Sam, time for the shock wave: a super

sound tsunami that blasted all before it.

MMMWWWAARRGHHH!

The sound wave broke from Sam's mouth

and boomed across the garden.

To Sam's surprise, though, these pumped-

up pigeons seemed to float on the sound wave,

like surfers riding a huge breaker. Pig, on the
other hand, got blasted into the bushes.

After that, the bird bullies lost interest and flew off.

Sam sat on his bed and thought about what he'd seen this morning: two separate pigeon incidents that showed the birds to be strong and mean. Worse of all, they seemed almost immune to his mega super-loud sonic wave. Sam didn't feel very "Super" about that.

A tap at the window distracted him. "What now?" he said, quite loudly (obviously).

A pigeon – again! It sat on his window sill, tapping lightly at the glass.

Sam was about to shoo it away, shout at it, send it packing, when he paused. It was smaller than the big bruiser pigeons, the ones

causing all the bother. It had dark feathers
above its eyes like handsome brows, and
something in those orangey-brown peepers
seemed to speak of a special intelligence. Then
Sam noticed the pigeon had something in its
beak.

Sam opened the window and stood back.
The bird hopped in and dropped the piece
of paper. Sam picked it up, unfolded it, and

found that it was the newspaper report that the backpack man had talked about yesterday: about how Sam had defeated his no-good teacher with the power of his voice.

"So you know who I am?" asked Sam.

The bird nodded.

Wait, what? Did it? Could it? Really?

Sure looked like a nod.

"What do you want?" Sam asked.

The bird didn't respond and Sam was about to ask again when Nina burst into his room.

"Let's go, Sam," she said. "The race starts in an hour!"

Nina and Sam were taking part in the Topside Festival of Fun "Fun Run of Fun", an annual event held before the ever-popular Topside Festival of Fun. Nina has knitted them some running socks specially for it.

Sam didn't move.

"What's that?" Nina gasped, suddenly spotting the pigeon.

"A pigeon," said Sam. "Obviously."

The bird sort of nodded.

"It seems friendly," said Sam. "Maybe it needs help."

"Reckon you need help, more like," said Nina. "Pigeons cannot be trusted, Sam – get away from it!"

"But this one seems different – and smart," said Sam, "especially compared to those other big, nasty pigeons I saw this morning, smashing into my window and duffing up Pig."

Nina shook her head impatiently. She pulled a knitting needle from her hair and aimed it, javelin-style, at the pigeon. The bird flew out of the window to avoid the speeding dart and Nina slammed the window shut after it.

"Now, we have to run – literally," she said. "We can talk about this later. Forget about the pigeons. Let's go."

Chapter 9
WHEN FUN RUNS GO UN-FUN

It turned out to be quite hard to forget about
pigeons, though, even at such a big and
exciting event as the Topside Festival of Fun
"Fun Run of Fun".

Over two hundred people, young and
not so young and a bit older, had assembled
in Topside Park to take part in the three-
mile race. Sam and Nina's sporty friend
Jock Wilson was there, of course, and their
classmates Agatha Ackerbilk and Aaron

Abacus were also running. The mayor of Topside, Mr Crackling, in his bright red robes and golden chains, made a boring speech which nobody could hear very well and then shouted, "On your marks, get set, GO!"

The runners surged off. Jock tore away at top speed while Sam and Nina settled into a comfortable jog. It was only after the first mile that Sam noticed the sun had gone in and a cold breeze was whipping through the park. He glanced up, and almost stopped in his tracks.

A cloud had passed over the sun, but not a cloud made of cloud, a cloud made of birds. Pigeons! A huge grey storm of pigeons, flying closely together and blocking out the light.

The other runners had noticed the birds, too. People were pointing and shrieking.

"Do something, Sam!" said Nina. "Remember who you are!"

I'm Sam Lowe, thought Sam. But then he remembered. *I'm SUPER LOUD SAM!* The pigeon cloud was heading for the crowd. It was time to act! Sam shouted in his hugest voice, **"STAY BACK!!"**

But the pigeons kept coming. They were flying low now. Sam could almost reach up and touch them as they passed over. The birds were big and powerful, and heading at top speed straight towards the runners.

"TAKE COVER!" bellowed Sam.

The runners crouched, covering their heads with their hands. Some of them hid under trees. But it was no use.

The pigeons swooped, low and straight and fast, and they pooped at exactly the same moment. A shower of ploppings rained down on the runners. There was simply nowhere to hide from this blizzard of pigeon poo.

SPLAT, SPLAT, SPLAT, it went as it struck the crowd, covering them in streaks of white and green.

The runners shouted out, groaned, rolled on the grass.

"Sam, you're hit!" yelled Nina.

Sam staggered around, trying to flick the icky gunk out of his hair, all the while looking up at the birds. They were circling above the park again. Were they going to launch another poop attack? Not if Sam could help it! This time he would try a shock wave. The biggest, most powerful wave of sound he had ever produced. He built up a huge rumble in his chest and then sent the wave of sound flying towards the birds. It blasted upward and Sam watched, eyes wide, as it hit them.

But then...

Nothing.

Instead of blasting the flying carpet of pigeons safely up and away, it simply made it ripple gently, like a sheet on a washing line. The ripple passed through the birds, nudging them slightly out of formation, but not slowing them down or scattering them. Sam was horrified! What had happened to his shock wave? Why didn't it work?

He stood and stared as the birds flapped ever closer, heading for the crowd again, until Nina rugby tackled him into a bush, shouting, "Get down!"

Then the two of them watched as the birds swept over the crowd for a final time, making everyone duck in terror. But there was no more poo and the birds simply cruised off out of sight.

Chapter 10
AFTER THE ATTACK

After the shock of the fly-by pooping, the runners in the Topside Festival of Fun "Fun Run of Fun" abandoned the race. They were no longer having fun. They no longer wanted to run. Not with pigeon poo clogging up their hair and decorating their shoulders. Plus, the paths were all skiddy now. Dangerous.

Everyone had been so stunned that they hadn't noticed Sam's booming shock wave as he tried to bring down the pigeons. They had been too busy hiding under trees and wiping plop off their faces.

Jock Wilson raced up to Sam and Nina. He had a big streak of pigeon poop down his front but was still beaming, in his typically positive way.

"Wow!" said Jock. "Messy! But I suppose when that many birds fly past, someone's going to get pooped on!"

"But *everyone* got pooped on," said Nina. She had taken off her knitted running hat, which now needed a wash, and was quickly knitting a clean replacement.

"It was no accident," said Sam. "Those

birds meant to do that. It was a planned attack."

Jock and Nina looked at Sam. Was he right? And if he was right, what did him being right mean? For now? For the future? For the people of Topside?

"There were just so many of them!" said Sam. "I couldn't stop them. I tried, with my voice, but I couldn't beat them back." He hung his head. A little drop of pigeon plop splashed down on to his top. Nina patted him on the shoulder kindly, and then stopped when she realized her hand was getting all pooey too.

"Come on," she said. "Let's go and buy some shampoo."

Chapter 11

PANIC ON THE STREETS OF TOPSIDE

The three friends hurried to the nearby supermarket and found it already full of runners grabbing soap and shampoo and washing powder. Sam and his friends joined the crowd in the bath-and-shower aisle and then heard shouts from the front of the store.

"Hey! What? Get out! Put that back!" someone was yelling.

Uh-oh! More pigeon pandemonium! A

handful of birds were pecking the guy on the checkout like his hair was full of seed – which it wasn't, it was just regular seed-free hair. Another two landed on the till, punched the keyboard with their beaks and made the cash drawer open. They then helped themselves to some ten-pound notes and flew off. Their bullying friends grabbed a packet of gum and some mints and also flapped away.

That was the final straw! A feeling of panic surged through the shop. The customers forgot about their purchases and ran out, staring at the skies as they scurried away.

"The pigeons have gone mad – mad, I say," one person yelled, and who could argue with that?

Not Sam, Nina or Jock.

"Let's get out of here," said Sam, booming above the noise of people shrieking and running. "But meet round at my house later so we can watch *Talking Topside* together! Something tells me pigeons are going to be headline news today."

Chapter 12

A PERSISTENT PIGEON

Back at home, safe from the swooping poopers, Sam caught his breath. He showered, put on clean clothes and was just relaxing on his bed when there was a tap at the window.

"Not you again!" yelled Sam, loudly and angrily. **"GET LOST!"**

It was the pigeon: the one that had shown Sam the newspaper article about his Super Loud antics. The one who understood English. This bird seemed to be a cut above the pigeons that had wrecked the fun run, but even so, Sam was in no mood for being generous.

"There is no way on this planet that I am letting a pigeon into my room after what has just happened," yelled Sam, staring at the bird through his window. "No way!"

The bird stared back, looking sad and worried. But that was impossible, wasn't it? Pigeons couldn't look sad and worried. Their eyes were beady, not needy.

Sam ignored the pigeon, but the pigeon stayed put. Sam read his favourite comic, *The Astonishing Col-Slaw Battles the Toxic Tortoise of Terror*. The pigeon didn't move. Sam strummed his guitar and sang along, really loudly (and out of tune – painful). The pigeon didn't budge. And so the day slipped away like custard down a plughole, with the pigeon sitting tight outside Sam's room and Sam sitting tight inside, until Jock and Nina showed up to watch *Talking Topside*.

Chapter 13
RUNNING REPORTS

Together with Sam's mum, they all sat in front of the TV. With a flinch of irritation, Sam noticed the pigeon again, now perched outside the sitting-room window.

"BOG OFF!" he blasted.

Sam's mum spat out a mouthful of tea in shock at the noise. No amount of being Sam's mum could make Sam's mum used to the noise that Sam produced.

"Sorry! I meant the pigeon," said Sam.

Talking Topside started. Newsreader Martin Streaky was sitting at the news desk with a picture of raggedy, splatted-on runners in Topside Park behind him.

"Their naughty antics have been hitting the news for a few days now, but today, pigeons showed us an even more sinister side," said Martin Streaky. "A fun run in Topside Park this morning was dive-bombed by birds which proceeded to poop all over the runners. Tess Trotter has the dump-down. Sorry! I mean 'lowdown'. Please be advised that Tess's report contains scenes that some of you may find disturbing."

The children and Sam's mum watched

silently, huddled together in a tense group.
The pigeon on the window sill also watched.
Here was reporter Tess Trotter in Topside
Park again. She must have got there soon after
Sam, Nina and Jock left. There were still some
runners looking dazed, hugging each other
and wiping themselves with tissues.

"It was supposed to be fun. A *fun* run. But
the run soon turned into NOT fun, and our
worst fears about pigeons came true," said
Tess Trotter, with her ultra-serious face on.
"This amateur footage was captured by a
spectator."

A shaky film, recorded on a mobile phone,
showed the birds swooping down, scattering

the crowd with their spray of plop. You could just hear the groans of the runners and then the film abruptly stopped. Perhaps the phone had been splatted on, too?

"Mayor Crackling was here today," Tess went on, turning to the mayor. "Describe what you saw."

Still wearing his red robes (now flecked with white pigeon plop), the mayor spoke solemnly, describing how the race had been attacked, bombed, pooped on, ruined, splatted, spoiled, trashed, wrecked and ended.

"How do you feel now?" asked Tess Trotter.

"I feel like I need a shower," said the

mayor, "and I'm worried about stains to my robes."

"Do you have a message for the people of Topside?" asked Tess.

"Yes I do. It is this. We must continue

our lives as normal," said the mayor. "We cannot let the actions of a few crazed pigeons intimidate us and spoil our peaceful, happy lives here in Topside. It is the Topside Festival of Fun tomorrow and I urge all Topsiders to come along, have a wonderful time and put all this pigeon poo behind them."

"Will you be investigating the incident?" asked Tess Trotter.

The mayor frowned. "I don't think so," he said. "These are just birds, after all. We can't very well interview them to find out their motives, can we?"

Suddenly, the pigeon sitting outside the sitting room began tapping on the window urgently. Everyone jumped and stared.

"Ignore it," said Sam. "It's a bit weird."

Tess Trotter was still speaking to camera when the pigeon began rapping madly on the glass again with its beak. And at that moment, Sam saw him: the backpack pigeon man from the warehouse. He must have been standing behind the mayor all along. Suddenly, his head popped out, he blinked at the camera, and then he was gone.

"HIM!" yelled Sam.

"Who?" asked Nina.

"HIM!" roared Sam, pointing.

"Oh!" said Nina, understanding.

"What?" asked Jock.

"Where?" said Sam's mum.

But Sam didn't answer. He got up and opened the window to let the pigeon in.

"What are you *doing*?" yelled his mum. "Don't let that filthy bird in here! It could murder us all!"

"Look at it!" said Sam, in a loud, stern voice, for he was having a big, serious thought. Some might call it a *revelation*.

He stared at the bird. It had a calm, intelligent look about it. Perhaps it was frowning a bit, too? Suddenly, it seemed obvious. As obvious as a red tail on a polar bear. As obvious as a streaker on a football pitch. This was no dive-bombing, cash-machine-raiding, pooper-dooper pigeon. This pigeon was different.

"It actually looks really sweet," said Nina. "Not like those big birds that cause trouble."

"Exactly!" said Sam. "It's more than just sweet. I see it now. It's trying to help. It's on our side. It can even understand English."

"Excellent!" said Jock, who said "excellent" a lot. It was his favourite word. It was just so excellent.

"Come on," said Sam. "I think we need to pay our friend in that warehouse a little visit. The mayor said he can't question the pigeons about today's attack, but we can question the man who trains them."

The pigeon nodded and climbed on to Sam's shoulder. With his new friend by his side, and his other friends also by his side, but not on his shoulder, Sam marched out of the front door.

Chapter 14

SAM'S SHOUTING SHAME

Sam, Nina and Jock walked quickly and silently. Down by the train station, a man was selling hats with little umbrellas attached. "Protect yourself from pigeons!" he shouted. "Stop the plop!"

The children carried on past him. As the warehouse came into sight, the pigeon became nervous. You know how a pigeon looks when it's nervous? Oh, you don't. Well, twitchy and jumpy, always peeping over its shoulder and looking up into the trees.

"You're worried about going to the warehouse, aren't you?" Sam asked the pigeon. "You think I might lose you amongst all those other pigeons and they could hurt you when they realize you're not one of them."

The bird nodded.

"We need to disguise you," said Sam. "Nina?"

"Already on it!" said Nina, her knitting needles a blur of activity.

Seconds later, she had created the perfect disguise: a knitted yellow canary suit! Now Sam would be able to spot his pigeon friend easily, but the other birds would not be able to

identify him.

Sam helped the pigeon put on the disguise

and the group approached

the warehouse. When they

were a few metres away,

the huge double doors

at the front swung

open.

"Good evening!"

It was the man with the backpack, sitting

surrounded by pigeons. In front of them, a huge cinema screen hung from the roof.

"So good of you to join us!" said the man. "We were just reviewing today's events."

Sam's pigeon friend began hopping up and down in agitation as the man flicked a switch on a remote control and fun-run footage played across the screen. Then the wobbly camera turned to show the face of the person holding it – it was the man! Of course!

The children gasped. The man paused the film and the pigeons all clapped, tapping their grey wings against their backs in fluttery approval. Sam stared. There were thousands of them, all bigger and tougher looking than pigeons should look. It gave Sam the heebie-jeebies.

"You filmed the footage that was on the news!" Sam said.

"But of coo-coo-coo-course!" said the man. "Let's watch it again! There may even be a few 'extras' that didn't make it on to the news!"

The film played again.

"Aren't they majestic?" said the man. "Notice how tightly they are flying together. Exquisite! All those other little pigeon attacks and silly nonsense were just a bit of fun. Now you can see what my pigeons are really capable of when they work together!"

The camera panned down to show the runners.

"Oh, look! Who's this?" said the man.

The camera swung round to Sam, who was valiantly trying to blast the pigeons away with his super-loud sonic boom. It zoomed in on his face, showing his expression turn to surprise and dismay when the pigeons kept going, despite the blast.

"WHY ARE YOu SHOWING US THIS!" exploded Sam, his cheeks hot with embarrassment.

The backpack man cocked his head to one side and gazed calmly at him. "I just wanted to show you how powerful my birds are!" he said.

"And remind you how insignificant you are. Your big shouty voice, all that booming... We all saw — it did *nothing*. You are not exceptional after all. I was mistaken. Super Loud? *Pooper* Loud, more like!"

Sam felt angry. Then ashamed. Then confused. What if the man were right?

Sam span round suddenly, remembering the locked room in the corner. **"WHAT ARE YOU UP TO IN THERE?"** he shouted, pointing at it. "What are you hiding? Let's find out, shall we?" He charged towards the room, through the pigeons, which fluttered out from under his feet. Then he sent out his biggest-ever shock wave, intending to blast the door clean off its hinges.

Only, it didn't.

The door rattled, but stood firm. Nina ran to Sam's side, putting a hand on his arm to stop him, but Sam shrugged her off and tried again.

VRROOᵒOMMM.

The shock wave rippled out of him like a sonic avalanche, but again, the doors did not budge.

"See what I mean?" said the man. "Your superpowers have met their match with me and my birds."

Sam was panting for breath now. "Who are you?" he yelled, feeling furious and upset and lots of other painful things.

The man strutted over, and then began

ushering them towards the door. "You ask a lot of questions, Sam," he said, "but you can only dream of their answers. Patience! All will be revealed – and soon! The town of Topside will echo with my name and worship my birds. But until then, fly away home, children, and take that thing with you."

"It's a canary!" said Nina, bravely.

"Whatever," said the man. "Get out of my warehouse. If I see you in here again, you will be sorry. You have seen what my flock can do today and that was just the start. Imagine if they got angry. Those beaks are sharp, you know. Think about that before you come rushing back."

Chapter 15
LOOK WHO IT IS!

Sam didn't speak on the way home. The pigeon, still wearing the canary suit, gently tickled his ear with its beak, but even that didn't cheer him up. He had been humiliated. His powers had let him down, and now it was certain: the backpack man had more pigeon mischief planned – and Sam had no idea how to deal with it. He longed to see Bryce Canyon again, his wise, cool speech therapist. Bryce would have some good Bryce advice, for sure.

But Sam had no idea where Bryce was now. *Forget it*, he thought, *I'm on my own.*

That night, a stream of terrifying nightmares unfolded in Sam's stressed-out brain. A giant evil hedgehog was about to pounce on Nina. Sam tried to shout a warning, but no sound emerged. Next, Jock was playing basketball, not with a proper ball – with a bomb! It would go off if he shot a hoop. Sam tried to force the ball away, but could not move it. Then Jock bounded up to the hoop, threw the ball up and...

"No!"

Sam yelled himself awake so loudly his ceiling light swung and his curtains flapped. He

sat up in bed, sweating and panting. He looked
around for the pigeon, but he was gone. Just like
Bryce, the bird had left without warning. Sam's
heart sunk. Surely, he could still rely on Jock
and Nina, couldn't he? They wouldn't abandon
him in his moment of crisis?

Sam stuck his head out of his window and
called in his giant voice to Nina and Jock, who
lived nearby.

"JOCK! NINA!" Sam
boomed. **"COME AND HAVE
BREAKFAST AT MINE."**

His voice was loud, but also wobbly. This
was a first. Sam clutched his hand to his
throat. Was he losing his voice? First his sonic

shock wave failed him, and now his super-loud voice? Maybe the man in the warehouse had been right. There was actually nothing super about Sam, after all.

Once that doubt had crept into Sam's brain, he could not get it out. He hid under his duvet, feeling miserable, until he heard a knock at the door. *That will be Nina and Jock*, Sam thought, climbing slowly out of bed.

He was wrong.

He opened the door to find Bryce Canyon standing there. **"WAAHHHH!"** boomed Sam. It was a super-loud explosion of glee and joy! That was more like it!

"Hey, buddy," said Bryce. "How's it going?

Haven't lost your voice, I see!"

At that, Sam burst into tears of happiness and relief and other stuff. He was so happy to see Bryce, but so worried about his voice failing him at the fun run and in the warehouse. All those feelings got mixed up together like veggies in a blender, creating some highly emotional soup.

"What's this?" Bryce asked, concerned. "Come on, let's get inside and talk."

And talk they did. Sam's mum made Bryce some coffee, ruffled her son's messy hair and then left the two friends to chat. Sam told Bryce about all the bad pigeons in town and how his voice did not seem to scare them.

"What about your shock wave?" Bryce asked.

"That doesn't work either," said Sam. "They just fly along on it, or bounce with it, but they aren't blown off course. I feel so powerless."

Bryce thought for a while before he spoke. "If your shock wave is not strong enough, you must find a way to magnify it. It's not just the strength and volume of your voice that counts. It's what you do with it and how you control it that matters."

Just then, there was a tap at the door. Sam had forgotten about asking Jock and Nina over. It must be them.

But when Sam opened the door, it wasn't his two human friends that he found, but his

tiny pigeon mate. It was sitting on the mat
with some more newspaper in its mouth. It
flew into the house and straight to the kitchen
where Bryce was finishing his coffee.

"Gregory!" Bryce shouted, sounding like he
was greeting an old friend.

Eh? thought Sam. *Who the who-who is Gregory?*

Back in the kitchen, the pigeon was sitting
on Bryce's shoulder.

"Gregory Peck and I go way back," said Bryce, indicating the pigeon. "I taught him English a few years ago. Pigeon English."

"So that's why he understands what I say," said Sam.

"Oh, sure," said Bryce. "Gregory can't speak, but he understands a whole heap. He can read and he's an ace spy, too. Nobody notices pigeons, and that gives him an advantage. If you want information, Gregory's your man. Well, your *bird*. I thought you two would get along."

"You sent him to me?" asked Sam, but Bryce didn't answer. He had got up and was putting on his long leather jacket.

"See you around, short stuff," he said, heading for the door. "Stay noisy, and remember who you are."

With that, Bryce was gone.

Chapter 16
NEWS JUST IN

Sam was still puzzling over Bryce's words, dazed from seeing his brilliant speech therapist mentor again, when there was another knock at the door.

This time, it *was* Jock and Nina.

"Sorry we're late," said Jock. "Took a detour to Café Teaspoon and bought some doughnuts."

The three friends tucked into their sugary treats and immediately went into a doughnut trance in which their sole focus became the doughnuts. The rest of the world seemed to melt away, until Gregory Peck brought Sam round by pecking sharply on the table.

Gregory had spread the newspaper article he had brought in his beak across the table. The pigeon hopped about and pecked at it again.

Sam read, his eyes growing bigger with every sentence. He even dropped his half-eaten doughnut.

TOPSIDE MAN SELECTED FOR GROUND-BREAKING SCIENTIFIC PROJECT, read the headline.

It explained how local resident Brian Moor

had been chosen to join an exciting new

project, to give humans the power of flight. It

was the brainchild of a famous businessman

called Rich Handsome (a fitting name, as he

was both rich and handsome). There was a

photo of Rich with his arm around Brian

Moor, and a quote from him saying:

TOPSIDE MAN SELECTED FOR GROUND-BREAKING PROJECT

"If our research and experiments work, Brian could be the first man to fly without the help of a machine."

Sam squinted closer at the image and a *PING!* went off in his brain, like an alarm of truth and realization. That was him – the backpack man, standing there with Rich Handsome! Sam checked the date. The newspaper was from five years ago. Yes, it was definitely the same man – not wearing a backpack, but absolutely him.

"So he was going to be the first man to fly?" asked Sam.

Gregory nodded.

"But how?"

Gregory shook his head. He didn't know.

"Where did you get this article? In the warehouse? Is that where you were last night?"

Gregory nodded twice.

"Nice work, Gregory!" said Sam, patting the pigeon gently on the head. "Bryce said you were the one to ask for information. Amazing!"

Nina and Jock had finished their doughnuts now and were coming back from their sugary trance. Sam showed them the newspaper article.

"But how come we've never heard of him before?" asked Nina, looking up after reading it. "If he was the first man to fly, he would have been in the news. He would be famous."

"Excellent point!" said Jock.

"Perhaps the experiments didn't work," said Sam. "Or maybe Rich Handsome ran out of money for the project."

"The day Rich Handsome runs out of money is the day I stop saying 'excellent'," said Jock. "Rich Handsome is a multi-billionaire. He invented electric-warming pants. They are bestsellers in Russia and Canada, and all the polar explorers use them. And he started a business selling bottled air. And he runs a network of triple-decker buses. And he manages that band, One Dimension."

Sam frowned. He wasn't thinking about

electric pants or bands or buses. He was trying

to work out how and why Brian Moor had

gone from hopeful hero and history maker,

to winged weirdo, commanding an army of

pigeons.

"Why don't you just ask him?" said Jock.

"Ask who what?" said Nina.

"Rich Handsome," said Jock. "Ask him what

happened. He's opening the Topside Festival

of Fun later on today with Mayor Crackling."

"Brilliant!" said Sam, his big, excited voice

blasting the last traces of doughnut sugar off

the plates. "Maybe we can catch him at the

Town Hall now? Let's go!"

Chapter 17

THE SEARCH FOR BRITAIN'S RICHEST MAN

With Gregory Peck flying alongside, Sam, Nina and Jock raced off for Topside Town Hall, office of the mayor and all things important in Topside.

But the mayor was not there. He had gone to meet Rich Handsome at his hotel, before the grand opening of the Topside Festival of Fun.

Sam asked the mayor's secretary, Miss Chop, where Rich Handsome was staying.

She shook her head.

"I can't possibly reveal where such a famous and wealthy man is staying," she said. "Do you think I'm an idiot? Although, between you and me, if I had as much money as Rich Handsome, I know where I'd stay – the penthouse suite at the top of the Topside Plaza!"

"Thank you *very* much!" said Sam, as the three friends zoomed off towards the hotel.

"Oh..." said Miss Chop, realizing what she had done. "Bother."

Five minutes later, Sam, Nina and Jock were outside the Topside Plaza hotel. Gregory Peck perched on the railings. There was a doorman wearing a long black coat and a cap. As the friends approached, he shook his head.

"Hop it, young ones," said the man. "We don't want little Herberts like you cluttering up this fine hotel."

Jock stepped forward, his handsome face deadly serious. "Now look here, my good man, my father is Rich Handsome and he is staying here and when he hears that you would not let his son, er, Maximillian, into the hotel, he will be furious!"

The doorman looked worried. "Rich Handsome's son, are you?"

Jock nodded.

"Where is he staying then?" asked the

doorman, trying to catch Jock out.

"The penthouse suite, of course," Jock snorted. "Now please, stand aside. I've brought him a fried egg from his own pet goose for breakfast. He always starts the day with one. I need to give it to him before it gets cold."

"Where is it then?" asked the doorman. "This fried egg you're on about?"

Jock was becoming impatient. "In my pocket and, no, I won't get it out and risk it getting cold just so you can gawp at it," he humphed, turning into a real diva. It was very convincing, but then Jock had always been good at acting (as well as sport, maths and just about everything else).

The doorman looked uncertain, but slowly pushed open the door anyway and let the children through.

Once inside, Sam, Jock and Nina paused. They had never been inside the Topside Plaza before. My, it was posh. The chairs had red velvet seats and gold legs. There were twinkly chandeliers when you looked up and a shiny floor when you looked down. Suddenly, the lifts went *ding* and out thundered Mayor Crackling and a crowd of town-hall types, bustling along beside him, looking extremely hassled.

"Where on earth can he be?" huffed the mayor.

He was marching past the three children

now, heading for the exit, when Sam shouted,

"MAYOR CRACKLING, CAN i SPEAK TO YOu PLEASE?"

Sam's loud voice made the mayor stop.

"Not now, son, I'm in the middle of an

emergency," he said. "Rich Handsome has

disappeared. He checked into the hotel, but

no one has seen him since. He is supposed to

open the Topside Festival of Fun later – if we

can find him."

With that, the mayor, full of worry and

stress, swept out through the revolving

doors. And back again. And out. And back

again. (His mayoral chain got stuck in the

spinning doors, and he had to take a few extra laps before he could wrench himself free and tumble out on to the pavement. Bit embarrassing.)

The children followed.

"Delivered your fried egg, then?" asked the doorman.

"Oh, er, yes," said Jock. "Thank you. It was still warm, so . . . great."

"I don't suppose you saw a man with a big backpack come into the hotel this morning?" Sam asked the doorman. "Walks with a bit of a strut like an overgrown bird?"

The doorman thought for a moment. He looked unsure, then he looked confused, then he looked like he had remembered something. "Yes, I know the man," he said. "He went in about half an hour ago. Hasn't come out yet, though."

Sam thanked the doorman and his

friends hurried away.

"Sounds like our friend Brian Moor from the warehouse has been here," said Sam.

"But where has Rich Handsome legged it to, when he should be getting ready for the festival?" asked Jock.

"It's obvious, isn't it?" Sam boomed. "The pigeon backpack man turning up at the hotel and Rich Handsome going missing. They are connected."

"How?" asked Jock. "Mr Handsome has left the hotel but the backpack man is still inside."

"Wrong!" said Sam. "They left together, just not by the front door. Think about it! When you have a gazillion pigeons to help you, there are other ways of getting down from a room at the top of a building."

Nina looked serious. "The man with many wings can achieve all sorts of things," she said.

"Exactly!" said Sam.

"You think Brian Moor has kidnapped Rich Handsome?" said Jock, stopping suddenly on the pavement.

"I'd bet my mum on it!" said Sam. "Those two go back a long way, but I have a feeling that Brian Moor has more in mind than a friendly catch-up with Mr Handsome. We have to find them – and fast."

Chapter 18

A DISCOVERY AT THE WAREHOUSE

Sam was not keen to return to the warehouse. Not after Brian Moor had threatened the children never to return. Not after failing to blow those doors down and being mocked. But Sam was sure Rich Handsome was in danger, and the first place to search for him had to be the warehouse.

Sam needed to be brave. He focused on what Bryce had said. What was it? "Find a way to magnify your voice."

The children were approaching the train station now, on their way to the warehouse on the wasteland beyond. *Magnify. . . ? Magnify. . . ?* The word spun around Sam's head; he was thinking so hard he forgot to check his footing and. . .

CRASH!

Sam walked straight into a line of traffic cones.

"Are you OK?" Nina asked. Gregory flapped above, concerned.

Sam grinned like he had never been better and picked himself up. But that wasn't all he picked up. Looking around to check nobody was looking, Sam grabbed one of the traffic cones and rushed off, with Jock and Nina running along behind and Gregory Peck flying overhead.

Once back at the warehouse, the children paused near the front doors. They half expected them to open, like the last time they had visited, but instead the doors were locked and the whole building had a quiet, closed-up feel. The children raced round to the small side window. It had been mended since Sam blasted it, but he easily blew it open again with a super-loud shock wave of sound. Using another rope knitted by Nina, the three friends shimmied up and in, with Gregory Peck, wearing his canary suit for safety, flying in behind.

The warehouse felt oddly quiet. No sound of pigeons scratching around in the rafters. No cooing. The whole place was empty.

"Where have all the pigeons gone?" asked Nina. "There are normally thousands here."

"And where are Brian Moor and Rich Handsome?" asked Jock.

There was a muffled cry. The three children looked at one another, eyes wide.

"It's coming from over there," whispered Nina, pointing towards the locked room.

"We have to get inside," said Jock. "Can you do it, Sam?"

They hurried over. Sam had failed to open the doors yesterday. Would he be able to blast them down today?

The visit from Bryce Canyon had filled up Sam's confidence tanks to the max. The dial on his internal confidence-o-meter was set to FULL. It was time to take Bryce's advice and magnify that shock wave.

Sam began to rumble, preparing a wall of sound. Just as he was about to let it go, he raised the traffic cone to his lips and blasted the wave through it. The cone worked like an amplifier, boosting the sound and hurling it forwards with extra force. The door rattle, strained and then clattered inwards, blasted clean off its hinges.

"WOO-HOO!" yelled Sam, marching over the collapsed door into the secret room. "That is how you do it!"

The muffled cries were louder now, coming from a distant corner. Sam edged towards the sound. "A light! We need a light," he called.

Jock searched near the entrance and found a switch. *Snap* – the room was suddenly bright.

Now they could see what was here. It was a lab, containing scientific equipment, test tubes, microscopes and huge fridges. It also contained...

"Rich Handsome!" yelled Jock.

There he was – Britain's richest man – crouched in the corner of the room, a scarf around his mouth, and his hands and feet tied with rope.

Sam quickly unknotted the scarf while Jock and Nina unravelled the bonds from Rich Handsome's legs and hands.

"Thank you! Thank you!" gasped Mr Handsome, struggling to his feet. His face, usually tanned from all his holidays to the Caribbean, looked pale and his golden hair was ruffled. Rich Handsome was shaking.

"Did backpack man do this?" Jock asked.

"Backpack man?" said Rich Handsome.

"Brian Moor, you know, the man who was going to fly," said Sam.

"Yes, yes, Brian did this!" said Rich Handsome, looking nervously past the children. "He tied me up then whooshed off again on his pigeons – but he said he's coming back!"

Chapter 19
LOOK UP!

Rich Handsome had barely finished speaking when a loud grinding noise, like machinery clanking into life, rumbled through the air. It was coming from above. Suddenly, a chink of bright sunlight ripped across the room, growing wider and wider.

Everyone looked up. A hatch in the warehouse roof opened to reveal brilliant blue sky. The children and Rich Handsome shielded their eyes and peered up.

When the hatch was fully open, there was silence for a moment, but then Sam heard something. The sound was faint at first, but even so, it made his stomach flip. Thousands of wings, beating at once, heading their way.

The three friends and Rich Handsome stood close together, staring up. Rich Handsome was shaking even more now. Gregory Peck perched on Sam's shoulder, his tiny pigeon eyes fixed on the open hatch.

"What is that?" asked Rich Handsome. "What's happening?"

But before anyone could answer, a blanket of grey blocked out the sun.

Chapter 20
A VILLAIN WINGS IN

If only the blanket of grey was an innocent rain cloud. Or a very large goose.

But no.

Sweeping overhead, cutting out the sun, was a huge flock of pigeons.

Sam watched in amazement. He could not see the whole flock or tell what size it was, but it had to be big. Really big. Like an alien spaceship cruising over a city. It took ages to pass overhead, before finally flying off to reveal blue sky again.

"What was that?" asked Rich Handsome, still confused.

Again, no time to answer. The flock was back almost as soon as it had left. The birds were circling above, like a giant pigeon hurricane. But instead of rain dropping from this cloud, something – some*one* – more sinister was descending. Brian Moor! Down he came, lowered by a chain of pigeons, until he was suspended just above the heads of Sam, Nina, Jock and Rich Handsome. His long dark coat had gone and in its place was a bright red suit that clung to his body with the huge gold letters "BM" across his chest and a shiny gold cape.

"Brian!" said Rich. "It's Brian Moor!"

"Wrong!" yelled the man, dangling above them. "I am Brian Moor no more!"

With that, the pigeons that had held him up released their claws and let him go.

Everyone below ducked, expecting Brian to crash to the floor, but instead, he hovered, slightly awkwardly, just above their heads.

"Coo-coo-coo-can't you remember, Rich?" the man said. "You gave me wings!"

With this, he whipped off his cape and sent it shimmering to the ground. Then he rotated in the air to reveal what he had been keeping in that backpack all along. Not an umbrella or a packed lunch or his mobile phone. No. Something far more odd, creepy and weird.

A set of wings! What? Yes, wings! Strange,
stunted wings, all wrong for the body they
were growing on, like the pointless tiny arms
of a T-Rex.

Nina gasped. Rich Handsome covered
his eyes and whimpered. Jock blurted out,
"Woooah, NOT excellent!"

Sam shuddered and blinked hard. So that was
what the backpack was all about. It was not for
carrying things, but for *concealing* them. And those
things were wings:
small, ugly wings
growing off the
man's back.

They were covered in a few fluffy white feathers, with pale pink skin visible beneath, like the wings of a balding chicken.

"Not very pretty, are they?" said the man, still hovering. "Not exactly what you promised me, Rich. I was going to be the first man to fly, with wings like a swan. You promised me fame and riches. But your experiments went wrong and you grew tired of me. You cast me out with nothing! I was alone – disfigured and abandoned!"

Brian Moor's tiny wings fluttered extra fast at this shocking information. He seemed to be struggling to stay up in the air.

"So I came to live here and met my true friends – the pigeons. They know what it is to feel overlooked and underappreciated. These birds love me, and in return, I have made them *magnificent*."

Again, the man's tiny wings seemed to be tiring. He dipped suddenly, making Nina and

Sam duck, and had to flap crazily to pull up again.

"But the pigeons are not magnificent!" said Sam. "They are horrible and mean. What have you done to them?"

"I have conducted my own little experiments, just like Rich Handsome did," said the hovering man. "I used my own blood plasma, which still contains traces of the experimental formulas used on me, to develop a band of huge, super-strong pigeons."

"So that's how they got to be so big," said Sam.

"Precisely," said the man. "My experiments were limited to Topside at first, but then I travelled the country, collecting pigeons from far and wide and modifying them, too. Now these birds will do what pigeons do best – fly home. Soon, the whole country will be full of my warrior pigeons, trained to cause chaos and destroy normal life. Pah! How I hate normal life!"

"Why are you doing this?" yelled Sam.

It was a good question.

"So that, finally, people will take notice of me. Finally, I will be famous – just as Rich Handsome promised. No one will be able to push me or my pigeons around again. Pigeons will become superior, humans inferior, and the one who is both human and bird will rule over all. That's me, by the way."

Brian Moor flapped hard again, hovered a little higher and then spread his arms wide.

"I shall rule the country and you will bow to my greatness. So forget Brian Moor. He is over. From today . . . I AM BIRDMAN!"

Chapter 21
BIRDS GO BAD

Nina, Jock and Rich Handsome gawped, speechless, as Birdman flapped above them, staring off into the distance, delighted with his dramatic plans.

But the silence was broken by Sam. He was clapping, slowly. Clap. Clap. Clap.

"Very nice!" Sam said. "That was quite a speech. We are all terribly impressed. I mean, what a story! Who knew? Incredible! I get it now. I really understand what's going on with this whole new villain identity. Catchy name, too. Nice. And that outfit – it's gorgeous! You know, red really suits you. You can so carry it off. But just to sum up – just to make sure we are all totally up to speed here – you are Birdman, right?"

The hovering man cocked his head. He looked puzzled.

"Well that's just peachy," said Sam, taking a big breath. "Because *I* . . . am **SUPER LOUD!!**"

Sam roared out his name. It felt louder than ever: a new top-volume triumph. Birdman shook his birdie head at the sound and his tiny wings flapped madly. But Sam was just getting started. He grabbed his traffic cone, and let loose an almighty shock wave of sound.

BOOM!

It threw Birdman upwards, his stubby wings beating frantically as he tried to regain control.

"Wingmen, help me!" Birdman shouted, and a flutter of pigeons swooped down, each sinking its tiny feet into Birdman's shiny red suit. They flapped together to hold him up as Sam released another, bigger blast.

KER-BOOM!

"Excellent!" yelled Jock excitedly. Rich Handsome was hiding behind him, shaking with fear. "Don't worry, Mr Handsome – Sam's amazing. He's Super Loud. He'll protect us!"

Sam's second shock wave threw Birdman and his Wingmen up towards the open hatch, but lots more birds quickly flocked to their master's aid.

"Take out the cone!" Birdman commanded, and more birds hurtled down, aiming directly for Sam. They began pecking his head and his hands; it felt like someone was hammering tacks into them.

"Ouch! No! Stop!" yelled Sam, swinging for them with the cone. Jock joined in, karate chopping the muscly pigeons, while Nina tried to poke them with her needles, but there were just too many of them and Sam dropped his traffic cone.

Instantly, the birds picked it up and flew out of the hatch. Now Birdman stared directly at Rich Handsome.

"Quickly, Mr Handsome, run away, get out of here!" Sam yelled above the sound of beating wings.

But it was too late. Another troop of strong, sleek birds swooped down, this time heading for the billionaire businessman. They flew so fast and so hard that Sam and Jock were powerless to protect him. The birds grabbed Rich Handsome and carried him upwards.

"Ca-coo-ca-coo-ca-come along now, Rich,"

said Birdman, still hanging in the air. "We have the Festival of Fun to open, remember? We coo-coo-coo-couldn't let the people of Topside down. Don't worry; I'll be happy to drop you off!"

Then Birdman and Rich Handsome were whooshed out of the hatch and engulfed in the vast cloud of pigeons swooping above. The sound of beating wings grew louder and stronger and, in a flurry of flapping grey feathers, they were gone.

Without wasting a second, Sam, Jock and Nina raced out of the warehouse towards Topside Park, venue for the Topside Festival of Fun.

"What a nut!" said Jock as they raced along.
"We can't let this Birdman fruit loop take over
the country with his evil pigeons."

"What are you going to do, Sam?" asked
Nina.

"Stop him!" roared Sam, loudly and
confidently. "But our first job is to save Mr
Handsome. He's in danger. I don't like what
Birdman said about 'dropping him off...'"

Chapter 22

PIGEON PANDEMONIUM AT THE PARK

After a few minutes of hard running, with Gregory Peck flying out in front, the children spotted Topside Tower. It stood at the edge of the park, rising grandly above the space, its shiny windows glinting in the sun.

"Almost there!" said Sam, pointing at the tower. "Come on!"

Despite all the pigeon attacks of recent days, there was still a huge crowd gathered in the park. They had come to enjoy the leech racing

and custard punching and cow tipping and
to hear local band the Topside Trumpeters.
They had taken the mayor's words about
carrying on life as normal to heart, but even
so, lots of people were wearing hats with
mini umbrellas on top, just in case the
pooping happened again. There
was also a stall selling various
bird-scarers, including
pocket alarms, deely boppers

with flashing lights, and hats in the shape of
sharks and bears and the prime minister, all
designed to put the pigeons off. It was doing a
brisk trade amongst the nervous Topsiders.

The children stared upwards. No sign
of Birdman yet. The sun shone down. The
sky was blue. The park looked beautifully
colourful. And the mayor, standing on
stage holding a microphone . . . well, he
looked rather red.

"I am sorry to announce that Britain's wealthiest man, Rich Handsome, is unable to open the festival today," said Mayor Crackling. "He has been called away unexpectedly and sends his apologies. But never mind! We have lots to enjoy here, so I now pronounce the Topside Festival of Fun – OPEN!"

The people clapped politely and wandered off, but before anyone could have a go at the guess-the-weight-of-the-sausage competition, or could watch the jelly-sculpting demonstration, a shadow fell across the park.

"Uh-oh," said Jock. "We've got company!"

People began looking up. A man pointed. "There!" he shouted. The mayor, still clutching his microphone, let out a swear word which the whole park heard.

The Topsiders gasped, screamed, clung to each other.

"What is it?" cried a little boy, unable to believe his five-year-old eyes, as an enormous grey cloud sped towards the park.

It was a huge flock of pigeons, of course, but unlike the flock that had menaced the fun run, this time it had a rider. Birdman!

The crowd could all see him clearly, standing on his flying carpet of pigeons, bestriding them like a mighty charioteer in his bright-red suit. His small, weird wings were visible, too, and so was Rich Handsome, a terrified figure, clinging to Birdman's leg.

Using reins to guide the birds, Birdman swooped his crazy carpet around the park several times as the crowd stared upward in horror. Then a single bird left the group, flew down to the stage and seized the microphone out of the mayor's hand, delivering it to Birdman, who began to speak.

"People of Topside, greetings from your new master!" he said. "Soon I will control the country with my army of loyal pigeons."

Then Birdman pointed at Tess Trotter

from *Talking Topside*, here with her news cameraman.

"Make sure you are filming this! I want the eyes of the world on me. They need to know who I am! In a moment, I will release this army of super-powerful birds you see me riding on. Like good homing pigeons they will return to the cities all over this land that they came from. Soon, my pigeons will occupy every corner of this country. They are trained to cause chaos and wreck human life, and only I can control them. So take notice of me. I am your leader now! I am Birdman!"

The crowd was silent.

"You were supposed to clap!" he scolded. "Fine. Why not cheer instead for the man who gave me wings? Let's hear it for Rich Handsome!"

There was no cheer, though, only more shocked silence.

"Oh dear, Rich, they don't seem that impressed," said Birdman. "Never mind, it was still worth your while turning up, because I am going to teach you a vital lesson today. A life lesson. It's time you understand how it feels to be dumped, discarded and . . ."

Birdman paused, before roaring, "DROPPED!"

With that, Birdman kicked his leg and shook

Rich Handsome free. Then the birds parted
and Rich Handsome began to fall.

"Quickly, Sam!" shouted Nina. "Do
something!"

Sam was already building
up a huge shock wave
in his chest. As Rich
Handsome plummeted
down, Sam blasted out
a wall of sound that
caught the tumbling
billionaire and whooshed
him towards the bouncy
castle. The wave hurled him
into the inflatable fortress,

where he pinged off the sides like a bullet ricocheting off a wall. He pinged up and down, side to side, over and over again, before finally coming to a stop.

Mayor Crackling bounced on to the castle to haul Rich Handsome off, and the two men boinged about, performing an awkward moonwalk until they reached the side and slid down on to the grass. It would have been funny, except it wasn't funny, because Birdman was still flapping above and threatening to rule the country. This could not be allowed to happen. Obviously.

"Sam, blast the birds away with your voice," Jock said. "Quick!"

"It won't work from down here," said Sam.
"But I have another idea. Nina – knit me a
rope!"

Nina's knitting needles sprang into action,
and seconds later, she handed Sam a woolly
rope.

"Now stand back," said Sam. "I'm going
up!"

Chapter 23

SAM TAKES THE RIDE OF HIS LIFE

Sam looped the rope and began to whirl it

around his head as though it were a giant

woolly lasso. As Birdman swept down over

the crowd, Sam

threw it into

the air as high

as he could. The

rope caught on a cluster

of pigeons and

instantly Sam was scooped off his feet and
dragged through the air behind them.

The crowd gasped as Sam went flying off,
dangling beneath the birdy carpet.

"You again!" fumed Birdman, peering down
over the side of his flying bird blanket. "Buzz
off, big mouth!"

Birdman pulled the reins and directed the birds towards the trees at the edge of Topside Park. The crowd gasped. Sam was about to be swung straight into their thick branches. But, just in time, he scampered up the rope and as the birds swooped back for another circle of the park, he pushed his way through a thicket of feathers and popped up on the top of the flying carpet.

"There he is!" cried Jock. "Go, Super Loud!"

Nina glanced up briefly then returned to her knitting.

Sam crawled across the flying birds towards Birdman. He grabbed at the reins, but

Birdman would not let go.

"Get off, you silly boy!" said Birdman. "Don't mess with my birds or I'll have them peck you to pieces!"

"No, you get off," said Sam.

More tussling. The birds were flying dangerously close to the trees again. The crowd held its breath. Tussle. Tussle. Tussle.

"I said . . ." repeated Sam, before opening his mouth as wide as it could go:

"GET OFF!"

It was a mega blast of sound. Stunned, Birdman fell backwards on to his birds, dropping the reins.

It was Sam's chance. He snatched them

up and yanked hard, sending the birds racing sharply to the right, away from the park and towards. . .

"Topside Tower!" said Jock. "They are heading for Topside Tower. Come on, Nina!"

The friends raced over. They could not guess what Sam was planning but they had to follow him.

Topside Tower glinted in the summer sun. It was the biggest building in Topside, a huge office block fitted with mirrored windows, and Sam was steering the birds right for it.

"He's going to hit it!" gasped Jock. "Is he mad? What's he doing?"

"Just a little closer," Sam muttered, as the

birds flapped forwards at top speed. "A little closer."

"What's going on?" said Birdman, shaking his head and ruffling his tiny wings as he came to and saw that Sam was driving his birds directly for the tower. "Stop!" he shouted at them, but they couldn't hear him.

Sam had begun to hum.

Of course, a hum from Sam could only mean one thing. He was brewing up another shock wave. It had to be big. It had to be bad. It had to be bold. Yesterday, Sam's shock wave had only rippled through the pigeons. This one had to do much more.

As Sam sped towards the tower, Bryce's

advice about magnifying the sound was ringing in his brain. He blasted out one epic, huge, monstrous wave of sound and sent it crashing straight for the tower. When the wall of noise hit, the mirrored windows seemed to bow inwards, but rather than breaking, they sent the sound bouncing back, bigger and badder than before. Now, this reinforced wall of sound and power was zooming straight at the pigeons, a force greater than anything Sam could have produced alone. It was a huge tsunami of sound and it was about to hit the birds head-on.

This time, the pigeons could not surf the wave of sound. This time, it did more than simply ruffle their feathers. This time, it barrelled through the birds like a bowling ball through chocolate fingers. Pigeons exploded outwards in all directions, spinning and spiralling sideways, up, out and, eventually, down.

They were not the only ones to fall. With the shock, Birdman was blasted off and landed in a tree. Sam, on the other hand, stunned by his own shock wave, was hurled high into the air. He flew up, up, up and then, almost in slow motion, he began to fall.

"Quickly, Jock!" yelled Nina. "Grab this and run!"

Jock ran, clutching the new piece of knitting Nina had been working on – a net! Gregory Peck flew in to help and Rich Handsome grabbed a section, too. The friends stretched the net tight and held it right under Sam, who was plummeting towards the ground.

"Pull hard!" shouted Nina. "Hold really tight! Here he comes...!"

Sam hurtled towards the outstretched net. Nina, Jock, Rich and Gregory braced themselves. The crowd held its breath and...

PING!

Sam hit the net,
bounced back up
into the air, did
a spectacular
somersault and
then plopped
down safely into the
woolly mesh stretched beneath him.

The crowd erupted into cheers and whoops
and clapping!

Woo-hoo!

It was over.

Chapter 24

NOW SAY SORRY

Sam woke to find a crowd gathered around him. Nina and Jock were grinning down at him, Gregory Peck was sitting on his tummy, and Mayor Crackling was looking happy for the first time in two days.

"What happened?" said Sam, still groggy from his own shock wave.

"You just saved the day, buddy!" said Jock. "You truly are a hero. Excellent!"

Sam rubbed his eyes, looked about him

and noticed Birdman, one hand cuffed to a policeman, who stood firmly on the spot. Rich Handsome was nearby, smiling instead of shaking.

Suddenly, Sam remembered it all. "Where are all the pigeons?" he asked.

"You stunned them with your stupid shouting!" Birdman spat, glaring at Sam.

"Shut it, Feathers," said the policeman, tugging the handcuffs.

"Quite right," said Mayor Crackling. "We don't want to listen to you and your crazy ideas any more. Your plans to gain power were despicable. You will never win fame, glory and respect by scaring people with pigeons."

"Maybe not," muttered Birdman. "I'd settle for an apology, though."

The mayor did not hear him. He had turned away, full of disgust.

But Sam had heard. "What did you say?" he asked, approaching Birdman and looking into his tiny birdy eyes. It was the first time Sam had looked at them properly. Far from seeing greed and evil there, he saw something else. What was it? With a gulp, Sam realized it was sadness.

"Maybe ruling the country and being a supervillain is not the answer," Birdman said to Sam. "Maybe, deep down, all I really wanted was for Rich Handsome to say sorry – for the experiments, for abandoning me, for these silly wings."

He fluttered his stunted wings a little and hovered a few centimetres off the ground, before the policeman yanked him back down to earth.

"Will you say sorry?" Sam asked Mr Handsome.

Rich Handsome, the country's richest man, walked up to Birdman.

"Sorry, Brian," said Rich finally, holding out a hand for him to shake. Brian Moor took it limply. "Sorry for all of it. I treated you badly. I see that now, and I want to make it up to you. I'll spend all the money it takes to rid you of those wings. How about a job working for me, too? Big salary, lots of pecks. I mean *perks*."

Sam thought Birdman might cock his head, birdy-fashion, as Sam had seen him do so many times before. But instead, Birdman's head fell. His shoulders sagged. His wings drooped. He let out a huge sigh.

The crowd were quiet for a moment, until a tiny figure muscled her way to the front.

"Now I should think it's time YOU said sorry too, Brian," said the woman.

This fearsome old lady was small, with a cloud of white hair on her head and a big handbag in the crook of her arm: the kind of handbag you could easily bash someone with.

"You have caused a lot of upset, my boy!" she said. "I couldn't believe it when I saw you on the news just now. That's what you have been up to all these years – hiding in a warehouse, messing about with pigeons! I wondered where you had got to. A fine way to carry on! Didn't I bring you up with manners? Apologize."

"Sorry, Mum," said Brian Moor.

"Not to *me*!" said the woman. "To all these nice people!"

"Sorry, everyone," said Brian Moor, looking very sheepish.

"That's OK," the crowd murmured back.

"Do you promise to give up trying to take over the country?" asked Sam.

"Yes," said Brian.

"And will you call off your pigeons?" Sam asked.

"Yes," said Brian.

"But how?" said Nina. "I thought they were trained to cause havoc."

"They are," said Brian, "but I can just tell them not to. They're really clever, remember?"

"Oh, right," said Nina.

"It seems we have a happy ending," said the mayor, beaming at everybody. "What say we return to the park and get this Topside Festival of Fun started properly?"

"Great idea," said Rich Handsome. "The ice creams are on me!"

And with that, the crowd let out a mighty whoop, scooped Sam on to their shoulders and marched back into the park. As the Topside

Trumpeters blasted out a celebration tune,
Brian Moor stood looking on, his tiny mum
beside him. She rummaged in her giant bag
and pulled out a sweetie, which she offered to
her son. He pecked it up.

"You need to work on that, too," she said.
"That's no way to eat. Manners, remember?"
Brian Moor nodded.

Chapter 25

A NIGHT
TO REMEMBER

Against all expectations, that year's
Topside Festival of Fun was the best ever.
Having been scared half to Brazil and back,
the people of Topside were now ready for
a party. After all, it's not every day that a
crazed half-man, half-bird threatens the
nation's safety, is it? It's not every day that a
young boy with a super-loud voice saves the
entire country from jeopardy. It's not every
day that it's the Topside Festival of Fun,

either... So for all this to come together at exactly the same time – well, it was just perfect, really!

Sam, Nina and Jock partied until they could party no longer, and were taken home to bed in Rich Handsome's private limousine. Rich stayed on at the park (he had taken a liking to Tess Trotter from *Talking Topside* and was buying her lots of hot dogs), and Gregory Peck was looking after Birdman's pigeons, who were still groggy after the shock wave and were recovering under some little bird blankets Nina had knitted.

It was late when Rich Handsome's luxury

car dropped Sam's friends, and finally Sam, safely home.

When the long black limo pulled up at Sam's house, the tall driver with a long scar down one cheek scooped the exhausted hero from off the back seat, knocked on Sam's door and passed the dozy child over to his proud mother.

Peeping sleepily over his mum's shoulder as the front door was just closing, Sam thought he recognized the driver as he strode back to the limo. Something about his height, his long leather coat... But Sam was too exhausted to work it out now and was asleep again before he landed in bed.

"Good night, Super Loud Sam. Until next time," murmured the driver, as he revved the engine and pulled away. "Have a great sleep. You've earned it."

Have you read the Pip Street books by Jo Simmons?

Read on for a peek at book one...

1

A Street Called Pip

Pip Street looks like an ordinary street, with houses that have doors and windows and roofs, and a bit of front garden at the front and a bit of back garden at the back. It smells like an ordinary street, too – that's to say, of not very much. Except on bin days, when it smells of mushrooms and warm nappies. But – and here's the shocking bit – it doesn't behave like an ordinary street.

No, because strange things are happening on Pip Street. Unexplained events. Mysterious mysteries. Funny stuff! And Bobby Cobbler is about to get caught right in the middle of it.

2

Here's Bobby Cobbler

Bobby Cobbler was a little boy, about
this big, with a sprinkling of freckles
and teeth as white as snow (and
everywhere that Bobby went,
his teeth were sure to go). He had
sharp eyes (but not sharp enough to
cut yourself on), and a mind as curious
as a kitten's and fifty times as smart.

Bobby lived on Pip Street. Actually, he was about to live on Pip Street. His mum and dad had bought a new home there. Nothing fancy. It wasn't a castle or a palace with golden toilets. It was normal size. Big enough for Bobby, his parents and his cat, Conkers. And for some furniture. And a fridge. And a bath. And some oven gloves. And for Bobby's DVD collection. He had the complete set of Custard and Chips, his favourite ever cartoon, and seasons one and two of Meerkats In Maidstone, in which a family of meerkats relocates to Maidstone.

Moving house is exciting, isn't it? But Bobby wasn't excited. Nope, he was cross. Grrrr, he was thinking. Bobby had lived in ten different houses and he was only eight years old. Even if you are rubbish at maths, you can tell that's a lot of moving. It's all because Bobby's dad was a travelling sweets salesman. Now that sounds cool, but it's not. For once Bobby's dad had sold his Ninny Drops and Milky Lugs and Sherbet Bumbums to one part of the country, he had to move again, to find new customers. Bobby would be just getting used to one school, just making friends, when whoops! it would be moving time again.

As the Cobbler car stopped on Pip Street,
Bobby reached for the basket next to him.
Inside, Conkers, his cat, was feeling cat sick,
which is like car sick, only for cats.

"Meow blurrrgghhh," said Conkers.

Conkers was as black as the devil's armpit with
shiny eyes, like torches down a well. If he had
been a human, he would have been a stuntman or
an international footballer who was also amazing
at playing the violin. He was just cool. Can pets be
cool? Yes, they can. Conkers was proof. Best of
all, Conkers always moved
with Bobby. Unlike the friends
Bobby had to leave behind,
Conkers was portable.

As Bobby and Conkers got out of the car, neither realized that they were being watched. And not just by the pigeon resting in a tree nearby. From a front room on Pip Street, nosy eyes ogled the new arrivals. Who was this mysterious peeper, staring at our new friend and his handsome moggy? And what was he or she muttering quietly? What's that you say, mystery peeper? What is it?

"Nobody does,
nobody does,
nobody does
a whoopsie
on *my* rug!"